My Weird School Daze #9

Mrs. Lizzy Is Dizzy!

Dan Gutman WITHDRAWN

Pictures by
Jim Paillot

HARPER

An Imprint of HarperCollinsPublishers

To Mr. Rafael T. Botello and his third graders at Brunswick Acres School in Kendall Park, New Jersey

Mrs. Lizzy Is Dizzy!
Text copyright © 2010 by Dan Gutman
Illustrations copyright © 2010 by Jim Paillot
All rights reserved. Printed in the United States of America.
No part of this book may be used or reproduced in any manner whatsoever without
written permission except in the case of brief quotations embodied in critical articles
and reviews. For information address HarperCollins Children's Books, a division of
HarperCollins Publishers, 10 East 53rd Street, New York, NY 10022.
www.harpercollinschildrens.com

Library of Congress Cataloging-in-Publication Data is available.
ISBN 978-0-06-155418-6 (lib. bdg.)—ISBN 978-0-06-155416-2 (pbk.)

Typography by Joel Tippie
10 11 12 13 14   CG/CW   10 9 8 7 6 5 4 3 2 1
❖
First Edition

Contents

1

The Lockdown!

My name is A.J. and I hate school.

It was Friday, one of my favorite days of the week. Do you know why Friday is one of my favorite days? Because the next day is Saturday. And then comes Sunday. And on Saturday and Sunday there's no school.

Yay!

My teacher is Mr. Granite. He's from another planet, but he's always talking about *our* environment.

"Always recycle your plastic bottles," Mr. Granite told us. "Because plastic bottles can be made into plastic lawn furniture. And plastic lawn furniture can be made back into plastic bottles. And plastic bottles and plastic lawn furniture can be made into plastic cup holders, so you can relax and drink from a plastic bottle while you're sitting on your plastic lawn furniture. And plastic . . ."

Mr. Granite didn't get the chance to finish his sentence because at that very moment the school secretary, Mrs. Patty, made an announcement over the loudspeaker.

"Attention," she said, "Dr. Emer is in the building."

"Dr. Emer is in the building!" shouted Michael, who never ties his shoes.

"Dr. Emer is in the building!" shouted Ryan, who will eat anything, even stuff that isn't food.

"Dr. Emer is in the building!" shouted Neil, who we call the nude kid even though he wears clothes.

"Dr. Emer is in the building!" shouted Andrea Young, this annoying girl with curly brown hair who I hate.

Everybody was freaking out!

"Who's Dr. Emer?" I asked.

"'Emer' is short for 'emergency,' Arlo!" said Andrea. (She calls me by my real name because she knows I don't like it.) "You probably weren't paying attention when they told us about Dr. Emer."

"I wasn't paying attention to your *face*," I told Andrea.

"It's a lockdown, A.J.!" said Ryan. "That's what it means when they announce that Dr. Emer is in the building."

Oh, yeah! Now I remember. Lockdowns are cool. Just in case a bad guy ever breaks into the school, we have to lock our class-room door, turn off the lights, sit on the floor in the corner, and stay really quiet until the lockdown is over.*

We all rushed over to the corner. Mr. Granite locked the door. He made us sit boy-girl-boy-girl so we wouldn't talk to each other. I had to sit next to Andrea Young. Ugh, disgusting!

"Everyone stay calm," said Mr. Granite.

We all sat without talking for like a million hundred seconds.

"Can we whisper now?" I finally asked.

"Okay," Mr. Granite said, "but quietly."

"I heard on TV that a crazy person

---

* Lockdowns are even cooler than fire drills. Fire drills are still cool because we get to stand around on the playground instead of learn stuff. One time I hypnotized Andrea, and she went crazy and pulled the fire alarm.

escaped from the loony bin last week," I whispered.

"Really?" whispered Emily, who is Andrea's crybaby friend.

"You shouldn't say 'crazy person,' Arlo," whispered Andrea. "My mother is a psychologist. She told me we should say 'psychotic.'"

"Maybe the psycho who escaped from the loony bin is inside our school right *now*!" said Michael.

"Maybe it's a *zombie* psycho," said Ryan.

"Maybe it's a zombie *cannibal* psycho," said Neil.

"Maybe it's a zombie cannibal psycho who eats kids for breakfast!" I said.

"Shhhhhhhhhh!" said Mr. Granite.

"Stop trying to scare Emily," whispered Andrea.

Emily is such a scaredy-cat. I bet she would have run out of the room if we weren't in the middle of a lockdown.

"We're all going to die," I whispered.

"I'm scared!" said Emily.

"Me too," somebody else said.

Sheesh, get a grip! It's just a lockdown.

"I have an idea," said Mr. Granite. "Let's hold hands. It will help calm us down. Everyone take the hand of the person sitting next to you."

Andrea looked at me.

"Hold my hand, Arlo," she said.

"No way," I said. "I'm not holding your hand."

"You *have* to," Andrea told me. "Mr. Granite said so."

I looked at Mr. Granite. He gave me one of those teacher looks.

I held Andrea's hand. Ugh, gross!

"Oooooh!" Ryan whispered. "A.J. and Andrea are holding hands. They must be in *love*!"

"When are you gonna get married?" whispered Michael.

"Shhhhhhhhhhhh!" said Mr. Granite.

Andrea kept looking at me and smiling.

"If we were married, Arlo, we would hold hands like this all the time," she told me. "Holding hands is so *romantic.*"

"If we were married," I said, "I would jump off a bridge."

"Oh, snap!" said Ryan.

"You're mean, Arlo!"

I had to hold hands with Andrea in the dark for a million hundred minutes. I thought I was gonna die.

And then suddenly, the door unlocked.

And then the doorknob turned.

"It's the crazy person who escaped from the loony bin!" whispered Ryan. Everybody was freaking out.

And you'll never believe who walked through the door at that moment.

Nobody. It's impossible to walk through

a door! Doors are made of wood. If we could walk through wood, they wouldn't bother putting up doors.

But you'll never believe who walked through the *doorway*.

I'm not gonna tell you.

Okay, okay, I'll tell you. But you have to read the next chapter. So nah-nah-nah boo-boo on you.

Crazy Week

The person who walked through the doorway was Officer Spence, our school security guard!

Officer Spence acts like he's a real policeman. But security guards aren't allowed to carry guns or beat up bad guys or do anything cool.

"It's all clear," Officer Spence announced. "The lockdown is over."

"Yay!" everybody shouted.

"Thank you, Officer Spence," said Mr. Granite.

"Just doing my duty, sir."

We all giggled because Officer Spence said the word "duty," which sounds just like "doody." It's okay to say "duty" in school, but you're not allowed to say "doody." Grown-ups get really mad. Nobody knows why.

"Did they find the crazy person who

escaped from the loony bin?" I asked Officer Spence.

"No," he replied. "That person is still at large."

"If they didn't find him, how do they know how big he is?" I asked.

Andrea rolled her eyes.

"At large means *'missing,'* Arlo!" she said.

"Your *face* is missing," I told Andrea.

"Oh, snap!" said Ryan.

"Don't worry," Officer Spence told us. "I've got my eyes open."

I hope so. It would be weird to walk around trying to find crazy people with your eyes closed. You'd bump into stuff.

Officer Spence makes no sense.

Mr. Granite went back to teaching us about recycling plastic, but a few minutes later there was a knock on the door.

"Who is it *now*?" Mr. Granite looked annoyed.

It was our principal, Mr. Klutz, and our vice principal, Mrs. Jafee. Mr. Klutz has no hair at all. I mean none. But when he poked his head in the doorway, he was wearing a long blond wig! Mrs. Jafee had one on too. It was hilarious.

"To what do we owe the pleasure of your company?"* asked Mr. Granite. "And

---

* That means "What are *you* doing here?" in grown-up talk.

what's with the crazy hair?"

"Next week will be Crazy Week at Ella Mentry School," announced Mr. Klutz. "Monday will be Crazy-Hair Day, so everybody should come to school with crazy hair. Doesn't that sound like fun?"

"Yes!" said all the girls.

"No!" said all the boys.

"And Tuesday will be Crazy-Clothes Day," said Mrs. Jafee. "Everybody should dress up crazy, you betcha!"

"Wednesday will be Crazy-Hat Day," said Mr. Klutz.

"Thursday will be Crazy-Shoes Day," said Mrs. Jafee. "And Friday will be Crazy-*Everything* Day!"

"We'll send a note home for your parents in your backpacks," said Mr. Klutz.* "But we wanted you kids to get excited about Crazy Week at Ella Mentry School."

---

* That's silly. Parents can't fit in a backpack. Except for really small parents, I guess.

"It's going to be one crazy week, by golly!" said Mrs. Jafee.

Like our school wasn't crazy enough *already*!

Crazy-Hair Day

Monday was Crazy-Hair Day. My mom put this stinky gel stuff on my hair and combed it all toward the middle to make a fake mohawk. She called it a "fohawk." It was cool.

Michael sprayed green dye in his hair. Neil the nude kid had on a baldy wig. He looked just like Mr. Klutz! Ryan put some orange stuff in his hair but left thin, dark lines in it so his head looked like a basketball. Andrea and Emily put colored ribbons and bows all over their hair.

Even Mr. Granite had crazy hair. He showed up with purple dreadlocks. It was hilarious. You should have been there!

After we put our backpacks away and pledged the allegiance, Mr. Granite said it was time for math. I hate math. Why do we have to learn math when there are calculators in the world? That's like walking ten miles to a store when you can take a car.

It's really hard to pay attention to math when your teacher has purple dreadlocks. In fact, it was hard to learn *anything* that morning because we were all looking at each other's crazy hair. My mohawk was itching, too.

After a million hundred hours, it was time for lunch. And then, of course, it was the best time of the day.

Recess!

Recess rocks! It's the only thing I like about school. We get to go out on the playground and do whatever we want. My friend Billy who lives around the corner told me that when you go to heaven, it's like recess all the time.

I went to play on the swings with Ryan, Michael, and Neil the nude kid. Andrea and her girly friends hung around so they could annoy us, like always.

So there we were, minding our own business on the swings, when this lady walked over from across the street with yellow hair. Well, *her* hair was yellow, not the street. It would be weird if streets were yellow.

Anyway, the hair on both sides of her head was curled up into buns like Princess Leia from *Star Wars*. It looked like she was wearing earmuffs. Or maybe she taped dinner rolls to her head. She looked weird.

"Hi kids!" she said. "My name is Elizabeth. But you can call me Mrs. Lizzy."

We told Mrs. Lizzy our names. Andrea

and Emily said they liked her hairstyle.

"Are you Princess Leia?" asked Michael.

"Are those dinner rolls taped to your head?" I asked. "Or are you wearing earmuffs?"

"Goodness no!" Mrs. Lizzy said. "This is my real hair."

"Did you do that for Crazy-Hair Day?" asked Ryan.

"No, I wear my hair like this *every* day," said Mrs. Lizzy.

If you ask me, she should cut her hair and get earmuffs instead.

"Are you a new teacher?" asked Andrea, who never misses a chance to brownnose a teacher.

"In a way, yes," Mrs. Lizzy told us. "The Board of Education decided that kids don't learn enough in school. So they started the 'Recess Enrichment Program.' That means you kids will get to learn new things during recess. Doesn't that sound like fun?"

"Yes!" said the girls.

"No!" said the boys.

What?! We have to learn stuff during recess? What's the deal with *that*?

Mrs. Lizzy told us boys to cheer up. She said that the Recess Enrichment Program will be fun and that she was going to teach us lots of cool things.

Bummer in the summer! It wasn't fair, if you ask me. Recess is supposed to be for burning off energy and running around. Nobody told us anything about a Recess Enrichment Program.

This was the worst thing to happen in my life since TV Turnoff Week.

4

An Important Life Skill

Mother's Day was coming up on Sunday. Mrs. Lizzy said that for our first recess enrichment project we should make something for our mothers.

"I'm going to cook my mom breakfast in bed," said Andrea.

"How are you gonna do that?" I asked.

"Do you have a stove in your bed?"

"No, Arlo!" Andrea said, rolling her eyes. "I'm going to make her breakfast on the stove and *then* bring it to her in bed."

"Oh," I said. "That's different."

"My mom loves to eat breakfast in her pajamas," Emily said.

"She should put her breakfast on a *plate*," I told Emily. "Your mom is weird."

Emily looked all mad, like she was going to start crying. As usual.

"No, dumbhead!" Andrea said to me, rolling her eyes again. "Emily's mom doesn't put the breakfast *in* her pajamas! She eats it while she's *wearing* her pajamas!"

I knew that. I just like yanking Andrea's and Emily's chains.

"Mothers like it when you make them a gift for Mother's Day," Mrs. Lizzy told us. "Today I'm going to teach you how to make the perfect Mother's Day gift."

"What's the perfect Mother's Day gift?" asked Ryan.

"A balloon animal!" said Mrs. Lizzy.

She pulled a long red balloon out of her pocket and blew it up. Then she tied the end and twisted the balloon every which way. It was really squeaky. The next thing we knew, the balloon animal was finished.

"See?" Mrs. Lizzy said. "It's a little doggie! Here, I'll show you kids how to make one."

Mrs. Lizzy's balloon dog was cool. It really looked like a dog. She pulled more balloons out of her pocket and gave one to each of us.

"Is it really important for children to learn how to make balloon animals?" asked Andrea. "Maybe we should use the Recess Enrichment Program to improve our reading, writing, and math skills."

"Can you possibly be more boring?" I asked Andrea.

What is her problem? Reading, writing, and math are way overrated. And balloon animals are cool.

"Think of it this way, Andrea," said Mrs. Lizzy. "When you grow up, you'll probably go on a job interview one day. What would happen if you were on a job interview and they asked you to make a balloon animal? If you had never learned how to do that as a child, you wouldn't get the job. That would be a shame. Unemployment is a big problem in our country. That's why it's so important for kids to learn how to make balloon animals."

Yeah! In her face! I love it when Andrea's wrong.

"And imagine if all the bad people in the world made balloon animals instead of committing crimes and hurting people," Mrs. Lizzy told us. "The world would be a much better place, don't you think?"

Mrs. Lizzy made sense. I liked her a lot. She also made great balloon animals. We all blew up our balloons and twisted them every which way.

"I worked my way through college by making balloon animals," Mrs. Lizzie told us. "I graduated with a degree in balloon animal construction."

"College must have been a lot cheaper in those days," I said.

Some kids from the other classes gathered around to watch us make balloon animals. It was cool.

Maybe the Recess Enrichment Program wasn't such a bad idea after all.

Crazy-Clothes Day

Tuesday was Crazy-Clothes Day. I wore my dad's pinstriped shirt, a red bow tie, soccer shorts, mittens, and knee pads. Knee pads are cool because you can flop down on your knees and it doesn't hurt.

"A.J.," Ryan said when he saw me come into our classroom, "those are the craziest

clothes I ever saw."

Like he should talk! Ryan was wearing his sister's dress, his mom's fur coat, and a pair of 2009 glasses that had the *00* go over his eyes and the *2* and the *9* on either side of his head.

Everybody was wearing crazy clothes.

At recess, guess who showed up at the playground again? Mrs. Lizzy, of course.

She was wearing a black plastic trash bag with holes cut out for her arms and legs. And she was carrying a bucket.

"Hi kids!" she said when she saw us.

"Hi Mrs. Lizzy!" we all yelled.

"Did you dress like that because it's Crazy-Clothes Day?" asked Andrea.

"No," she replied, "I always dress like this on Tuesdays."

That was weird.

But if you think

that was weird, you'll never believe in a million hundred years what Mrs. Lizzy brought with her to the playground.

I'm not gonna tell you.

Okay, okay, I'll tell you.

It was a goat!

She had a goat with her! And it was on a leash!

"Where did you get that goat, Mrs. Lizzy?" asked Michael.

"From Rent-A-Goat," she told us. "You can rent anything. This is my friend Pootie. Goats are my favorite animals. Do you kids have pets at home?"

"I have a ferret named Wiggles," said Neil the nude kid.

(Last year on Presidents' Day, Neil brought Wiggles to school. Wiggles escaped from his cage, got lost, climbed onto Emily's head, and was elected president of the school. That was weird.)

"I have a dog and some fish," I said. "It's my job to feed the fish. But one time a fish jumped out of the tank and my dog ate it. That night my mom asked me if I fed the fish and I told her that I fed the fish to the dog. I wasn't too upset when my dog ate my fish, because at least my fish didn't eat my dog. That would have been weird."

Everybody laughed even though I didn't say anything funny.

"Well, today for recess enrichment we're

going to learn another important life skill," Mrs. Lizzie told us. "I'm going to teach you how to milk Pootie the goat."

What?!

"Naaaaaaayyyyy," said Pootie.

"Milk comes out of goats?" I asked. "I thought milk came out of cows."

"It comes out of goats, too, Arlo," said Andrea. Little Miss Know-It-All was proud of herself because she knew something I didn't know. I hate her.

"See, we learned something already," said Mrs. Lizzy. "Goats give milk."

"I have a question," said Andrea.

"Yes?"

"Is it really important for us to learn how

to milk a goat?" Andrea asked. "I thought the Recess Enrichment Program was for us to learn how to do useful things, like use a camera, play musical instruments, or do arts and crafts projects."

"That's an excellent question, Andrea," said Mrs. Lizzy. "But what if you were playing in the playground one day and a goat wandered over? And what if the goat needed to be milked? And what if you had never learned how to milk a goat? That would be a shame. The poor goat wouldn't get milked. That's why this is so important. You never know when you might have to milk a goat."

"Naaaaaaayyyyy," said Pootie.

I really didn't think there was much

chance that a goat was going to wander over to our playground. But I wasn't complaining, because Mrs. Lizzy told Andrea she was wrong. So nah-nah-nah boo-boo on Andrea. It was the greatest day of my life.

"Okay," Mrs. Lizzy said, getting down on her knees, "this is how you milk a goat."

Mrs. Lizzy put her bucket under Pootie. Then she grabbed Pootie's udder and started pulling on it every which way. It looked like she was going to make it into a balloon animal! But Pootie didn't seem to mind. Soon milk started coming out, and Mrs. Lizzy squirted it into the bucket.

"Ew, disgusting!" I said.

"Naaaaaaayyyyy," said Pootie.

We were all giggling and making rude remarks and pretending to throw up. Emily couldn't even watch.

"This is hard on my knees," Mrs. Lizzy said. "How about one of you takes over and milks Pootie?"

None of us wanted to milk Pootie. I looked at the ground. Ryan looked at the ground. Neil looked at the ground. Even *Andrea* looked at the ground. If you don't want the teacher to call on you, always look at the ground. That's the first rule of being a kid.

"A.J.," Mrs. Lizzy said, "you're wearing knee pads. How about *you* milk Pootie?"

"Yeah!" everybody agreed.

"That's a great idea!" said Michael. "A.J. should milk Pootie. He's got knee pads."

I knew the only reason Michael thought it was a great idea for me to milk Pootie was because *he* wouldn't have to milk Pootie.

That's the last time I wear knee pads to school.

I got down on my knees. Mrs. Lizzy showed me how to take Pootie's udders and yank on them to squirt the milk into the bucket. I'm not going to bore you with all the details. But it was disgusting. I thought I was gonna throw up. Pootie didn't complain, though. She seemed happy to get milked.

"So, what do you think, A.J.?" asked Mrs. Lizzy. "Isn't milking a goat fun?"

"I think I'll never drink milk again," I told her.

"Arlo, you probably never drink milk *anyway*," Andrea said, rolling her eyes.

"I do too," I said. "I have Milk Duds and Milky Way bars all the time. They have milk in them."

Why can't a goat fall on Andrea's head?

Crazy-Hat Day

Wednesday was Crazy-Hat Day. Usually we're not allowed to wear hats in school. We were at recess one day and I asked everybody why.

"Hats might spread germs," Andrea said.

"Maybe the teachers are afraid we

would hide stuff in our hats," said Ryan.

"Like what?" asked Michael.

"Like a mouse," said Neil.

"Who's gonna hide a mouse in their hat?" I asked.

"A few years ago," Neil said, "I heard about some kid who hid his mouse in his hat and brought it to school."

"So just because some weird kid hid his mouse in his hat, that means *nobody* can ever wear hats in school?" I asked. "That doesn't make sense. What if that kid hid his mouse in his pants? Would they say we can't wear pants to school? Would we have to come to school in our underwear?"

"Nobody hides mice in their pants, Arlo!" said Andrea.

"Well, nobody hides them in their hat either," I told her.

Anyway, for Crazy-Hat Day I wore a hat with a little propeller on the top. Michael wore his football helmet. Ryan wore a pirate hat. Neil the nude kid wore an army helmet with leaves attached to it. Andrea wore a hat with pieces of fruit piled on top of it. Emily wore a stuffed animal on her head. Everybody had on crazy hats.

The only bad thing was that it was raining outside. That meant we had to have

indoor recess, in our classroom. Bummer in the summer! Indoor recess is no fun at all because we don't get to run around.

Mr. Granite told us that Mr. Klutz was going to come and keep an eye on us while he went to the teachers' lounge to eat lunch. He said we should be on our best behavior while he was gone. So as soon as he left the room, Ryan and I got up and shook our butts at the class. Most of the kids laughed.

My friend Billy who lives around the

corner told me that the teachers' lounge is a secret, magical world where the teachers play pin the tail on the donkey and swim in hot tubs and watch big-screen TVs. But when I went in there once, the teachers were just sitting around eating lunch. I think maybe they heard I was coming so they quick got rid of the hot tub and the TV so I wouldn't know they were having so much fun.

While we were waiting for Mr. Klutz to show up, guess who came into our classroom?

It was Mrs. Lizzy!

She was holding an accordion and wearing one of those green Robin Hood hats with a feather sticking out of the top.

"Hi boys and girls!" she said.

"Hi Mrs. Lizzy!"

"Did you wear that for Crazy-Hat Day?" asked Emily.

"No," she said. "I always wear this hat on Wednesdays."

"What are you going to teach us today for recess enrichment?" asked Michael.

"Today I'm going to teach you how to yodel," Mrs. Lizzy said.

"Yodel?" I asked. "What's that?"

"Yodeling is a kind of singing," said Little Miss I-Know-Everything. Andrea keeps a dictionary on her desk so she can look up words and show everybody how smart she is.

"That's right, Andrea," said Mrs. Lizzy. "Yodeling was developed in Switzerland as a way for people to communicate on mountain peaks. It sounds like this. . . . *Yo-de-lay-hee-hoo*!"

I never heard anybody sing like *that* before. It was the weirdest kind of singing in the history of the world.

"I can even yodel with my mouth closed," said Mrs. Lizzy. Then she started yodeling with her mouth closed.

"Mrs. Lizzy, is it really important for us to learn how to yodel?" asked Andrea.

"Sure!" said Mrs. Lizzy. "What if you were on a reality TV show and you had to yodel to win a million dollars. But you didn't know how. And because you didn't know how to yodel, you didn't win a million dollars. That would be a shame. That's why it's so important for kids to learn how to yodel."

Mrs. Lizzy threw back her head and started in yodeling. It sounded like this. . . .*

"Yodel-adle-eedle-idle. Yodel-adle-

---

* If you're reading this book with a parent or teacher, tell them to do the yodeling part. It will be hilarious.

eedle-idle-oo! Yo-yo yodel-laydee-hoo yodel-laydee-hoo, yo-yo yodel-yodel-laydee, yo-yo yodel-yodel-laydee-hoo. Yodel-leh-hee yodel-leh-hee yodel-leh-hoo. Yodel leh-hee yodel-lee-eee-ooo. Yodel-leh-hee yodel-leh-hee yodel-leh-hoo. Yada-yada yada-yada yad-eee-ooo, yippee odelay dee ahdelay ayaayayayay ohohohoh ladelayhee tee rodeo hee hee."

Yodeling is weird. Mrs. Lizzy sounded like my dad when he gargles in the morning. We were all giggling and poking each other with our elbows so we wouldn't laugh.

While Mrs. Lizzy was in the middle of

her yodeling, you'll never believe who walked into the door.

Nobody, because if you walked into a door it would hurt. But you'll never believe who walked into the *doorway*.

It was Mr. Klutz!

Mrs. Lizzy looked at Mr. Klutz and stopped in the middle of her yodel. Mr. Klutz looked at Mrs. Lizzy. I looked at Michael. Michael looked at Ryan. Andrea looked at Emily. Everybody was looking at each other. We were all afraid that Mr. Klutz would be mad. It was so quiet in the class, you could hear a pin drop.*

---

*Actually, you *can* hear a pin drop. Somebody dropped a pin one time, and I heard it.

"Was somebody yodeling in here?" asked Mr. Klutz.

"Yes!" said Ryan. "Mrs. Lizzy is teaching us how to yodel so we can win a million dollars on a reality TV show."

"I *love* yodeling!" said Mr. Klutz. "In my younger days, I spent a year in the Swiss Alps. I yodeled all the time."

"You yodeled all the time for a year?" I asked. "Didn't you get tired?"

"Not at all," he said. "I love to yodel."

And then he started in yodeling. . . .

"Yodel-adle-eedle-idle. Yodel-adle-eedle-idle. Yodel-adle-eedle-idle-oo! Yo-yo yodel-laydee-hoo yodel-laydee-hoo, yodel-laydee-hoo, yodel-laydee-hoo."

Mr. Klutz started dancing around, clapping his hands, and slapping his knees while he yodeled. We all got up and started dancing around, yodeling, clapping our hands, and slapping our knees. Then Mrs. Lizzy joined in, yodeling, dancing, clapping, and slapping her knees. *Then* she started hitting Mr. Klutz's head like it was a bongo drum while she yodeled. It was a real Kodak moment.

Does stuff like that happen at *your* school?

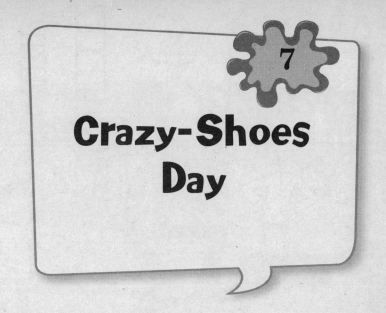

Crazy-Shoes Day

Thursday was Crazy-Shoes Day. Neil the nude kid had on army boots. Emily wore her mother's bunny slippers. I put two old shoe boxes on my feet. Everybody came to school with crazy shoes.

During recess Mrs. Lizzy came to the playground again. She had tennis rackets

strapped to her feet.

"Did you wear those for Crazy-Shoes Day?" we asked her.

"No," Mrs. Lizzy said. "On Thursdays I always wear tennis rackets on my feet."

Mrs. Lizzy is dizzy!

"What are you gonna teach us today?" asked Ryan.

"Today I'm going to teach you how to make fart noises with your armpits," Mrs. Lizzy announced.

What?! This lady was *cool*!

I already knew how to make fart noises with my armpits. *All* boys know how to do that. But Mrs. Lizzy was *really* good at it. She could even change notes! She played "Mary Had a Little Lamb" on her armpits. It was amazing. You should have been there!

The girls were not impressed with Mrs. Lizzy's musical-armpit ability.

"That's gross!" Emily said.

"Why would anyone *ever* need to know how to do that?" asked Andrea.

"Well, what if you were locked in a room," Mrs. Lizzy asked Andrea, "and you were tied to a chair. And you couldn't escape no matter how hard you tried. If you could make a fart noise with your armpits, somebody might hear it and send help."

"Couldn't I just yell and scream to get help?" Andrea asked.

"Not if they tied a rag over your mouth," said Mrs. Lizzy. "That's why it's so important for kids to learn how to make fart noises with their armpits."

"I still say it's gross," Emily said.

"We're not doing that," said Andrea.

"I just hope you never get locked in a room and tied to a chair with a rag over your mouth," Mrs. Lizzy told the girls.

Mrs. Lizzy taught the guys and me how to play "Yankee Doodle Dandy" on our armpits. For some of the notes she used the backs of her knees. It was cool. Then Mrs. Lizzy said she had to go but told us to keep practicing our armpit farts if we wanted to get really good at it.

"We will!" we promised. We started practicing right away.

Emily and Andrea said it was gross. They went off to go play on the slide. That's when I got the greatest idea in the history of the world.

"Hey, any time you want girls to go away," I told the guys, "all you have to do is make armpit farts!"

"You're right!" Ryan said. "As soon as we started making armpit farts, they left!"

"A.J., you're a genius!" Michael told me.

"No wonder you're in the gifted and talented program," said Neil the nude kid.

I should get the No Bell Prize for figuring out how to get rid of annoying girls. That's a prize they give to people who don't have bells.

Crazy-Everything Day

Friday was Crazy-Everything Day. I wore a bucket on my head and bounced to school on a pogo stick. Ryan wrapped himself in toilet paper. Michael attached bike horns all over his clothes and beeped them when he moved. Neil wore flip-flops and a hockey mask, and he carried a flyswatter in one hand and a banana in the other.

This had to be the craziest day in the history of the world!

Mr. Granite spent the whole morning trying to teach us stuff, but it was useless. Nobody could pay attention. Finally it was lunchtime and we got to go to the vomitorium.

The guys and me sat at one table, and Andrea and her girly friends sat at the next one. We tried making armpit farts to get rid of them, but they wouldn't leave.

Michael was eating a Lunchable. Ryan had soup in a thermos. I was eating a jelly and peanut butter sandwich. I used to eat peanut butter and jelly sandwiches, but

my mom said I couldn't have the same lunch every single day, so I told her to make me a jelly and peanut butter sandwich instead.*

"I wonder what Mrs. Lizzy is gonna teach us today," Michael said.

"Something weird, that's for sure," said Ryan.

"That lady has way too much time on her hands," said Neil the nude kid.

"Maybe Mrs. Lizzy isn't our recess enrichment teacher at all," I told the guys. "Did you ever think of that?"

"What do you mean, A.J.?" asked Michael.

---

* The difference is that you put the jelly on first.

"Well, maybe she kidnapped our *real* recess enrichment teacher and has her tied up in a secret room in the basement of the school. Stuff like that happens all the time, you know."

"You say that about *everybody*, Arlo," said Andrea at the next table.

"I do not."

"Do too."

We went back and forth like that for a while. But nobody wanted to hang around the vomitorium. We rushed through our lunch so we could see Mrs. Lizzy on the playground.

She looked crazier than *ever*! She had a spaghetti strainer on her head and a Ping-Pong paddle hanging from her neck, and she was carrying a big box.

"Hi Mrs. Lizzy!" we all yelled. "What's in the box?"

"Worms!" Mrs. Lizzy exclaimed as she opened the box to show us.

"Worms?!" we all yelled.

"Ew, disgusting!" said Emily.

"Are we going fishing today?" asked Andrea.

"No, we're going worm composting!" Mrs. Lizzy said.

Even Andrea didn't know what that meant. But Mrs. Lizzy told us that you can use worms to turn food scraps into this stuff called compost that can be added to soil to grow plants, flowers, fruits, and vegetables.

"The worms eat your leftovers and turn it into worm poop," Mrs. Lizzy explained. "It helps things grow."

"Ew, disgusting!" we all said.

"We're supposed to put worm poop on our vegetables and then eat them?" Ryan asked. Ryan will eat anything. One time he ate a piece of the cushion on the school bus. But I don't think he would eat something that was grown in worm poop.

"Yes!" Mrs. Lizzy said. "Worm poop makes a great natural fertilizer. And all you have to do . . ."

She didn't have the chance to finish her sentence because at that very moment the most amazing thing in the history of the world happened. Officer Spence came running over.

"Freeze, dirtbag!" he yelled, pointing his finger at Mrs. Lizzy just like they do on TV cop shows. "You're under arrest!"

WHAT?!

Suddenly, five guys in dark blue uniforms and sunglasses came running over. They surrounded Mrs. Lizzy.

"WOW," we all said, which is "MOM" upside down.

"Put your hands in the air, lady," Officer Spence ordered Mrs. Lizzy. "And don't try any funny stuff!"

Mrs. Lizzy put her hands in the air even though Officer Spence didn't actually have a gun. It was cool.

"Why are you arresting Mrs. Lizzy?" asked Andrea. "She didn't do anything wrong. She's our recess enrichment teacher!"

"No she's not," Officer Spence said. "She's just *pretending* to be your recess enrichment teacher. This woman is actually . . . the crazy lady who escaped from the loony bin last week!"

"Gasp!" everybody gasped.

"That's not true!" Mrs. Lizzy yelled.

"Oh, yes it is," Officer Spence insisted. "Mrs. Lizzy—or whatever her name is—kidnapped your *real* recess enrichment teacher and tied her up in a secret room in the basement of the school!"

"That's a lie!" Mrs. Lizzy yelled.

"Oh, yeah?" Officer Spence said. "Go get her, boys."

The guys with the sunglasses ran into the

school and came back out carrying a lady who was tied to a chair. Officer Spence took off the rag that was tied over her mouth.

"Ma'am," he said, "would you mind telling these kids who you are?"

"I'm Mrs. Sanford," the lady said. "I was on my way to school on Monday to start the Recess Enrichment Program when that woman kidnapped me! She tied me up

in a secret room in the basement of the school!"

"WOW!" everybody said.

"I did not!" said Mrs. Lizzie.

"You did too!"

They went back and forth like that for a while.

"See?" I said to Andrea. "I *told* you Mrs. Lizzy kidnapped our recess enrichment teacher and had her tied up in a secret room in the basement of the school!"

"Does this mean we've been taking recess enrichment classes from a psycho cannibal zombie who eats kids for breakfast?" asked Ryan.

"Can you untie me now?" asked Mrs.

Sanford, the lady who was tied to the chair.

"In a minute," Officer Spence told her. "I want Mr. Klutz to see this."

While Officer Spence was putting handcuffs on Mrs. Lizzy, Mr. Klutz and Mrs. Jafee came running over.

"What's going on here?" asked Mr. Klutz.

"Remember that crazy person who escaped from the loony bin last week?" Officer Spence said. "Well, here she is! Mrs. Lizzy is an imposter. She has been posing as the recess enrichment teacher all week."

Mr. Klutz turned to face Mrs. Jafee.

"Didn't you hire this woman to teach recess enrichment?" he asked.

"No, I thought you hired her," said Mrs. Jafee.

"I didn't hire her."

"Well, neither did I."

"Nobody hired her," Officer Spence told them. "She just showed up on Monday and told everybody she was the recess enrichment teacher. She's been teaching the children ridiculous things like how to milk goats and make armpit farts."

"Those are important things to know!" yelled Mrs. Lizzy.

"Quiet, you!" said Officer Spence.

"And who is *this* woman tied to the

chair?" asked Mr. Klutz.

"I'm the *real* recess enrichment teacher," said Mrs. Sanford. "I was going to teach the children useful things like how to use a camera, play musical instruments, and do arts and crafts projects."

"Did you try to escape when you were tied up in the basement?" Ryan asked Mrs. Sanford.

"How could I escape?" she replied. "I was tied to a chair! And I couldn't yell because there was a rag over my mouth!"

"You could have made armpit farts," I suggested. "Somebody would have heard them and rescued you."

"Or you could have yodeled with your

mouth closed," suggested Michael. "That's what I would have done."

"I don't know how to yodel or make armpit farts!" said Mrs. Sanford.

"Too bad," said Neil. "If you had learned that stuff as a kid, none of this would have happened."

"Are you blaming *me* for getting kidnapped?" asked Mrs. Sanford. "Untie me right now! I will never teach at this school again."

"You haven't taught here *yet*," Mrs. Jafee told her. "We'll untie you in a minute."

"I checked up on Mrs. Lizzy," said Officer Spence. "She's wanted in thirty states. She goes from school to school pretending to be a teacher. But she never got a teaching certificate. She's a phony."

"Oh, snap!" said Ryan.

"I just assumed she was one of our teachers," said Mr. Klutz. "I mean, she showed up every day with crazy hair, crazy clothes, a crazy hat, and crazy shoes."

"That's because she's *crazy*!" Officer Spence yelled. "And she picked the perfect week to come to our school. Nobody noticed how crazy she was because it was Crazy Week."

Wow! I always thought there were a lot of crazy teachers in our school, but this is the first time one was *really* crazy. And we got to see it live and in person.

"Good work, Officer Spence!" said Mr. Klutz.

"Just doing my duty, sir."

We all giggled because Officer Spence said "duty." I think he should get the No Bell Prize for figuring out that Mrs. Lizzy wasn't a real teacher.

"Take her away, boys," Officer Spence said.

"I want to teach! I want to teach!" Mrs. Lizzy shouted as they dragged her away. "The children must learn how to yodel. Get your hands off my worms!"

"Don't worry, Mrs. Lizzy," Mrs. Jafee said. "We'll get you the help that you need, you betcha."

"I say they should lock her up and throw away the key," said Officer Spence.

"Why would they do that?" I told him. "Then they won't be able to unlock the lock."

"That's the *idea*, Arlo!" Andrea said, rolling her eyes.

"They could make a new key," I told Andrea.

"You shouldn't throw away keys," said Emily. "Keys can be recycled."

We watched as the guys with sunglasses put Mrs. Lizzy and her worms into a patrol car. She was yelling something about balloon animals.

Every Week Is Crazy Week

I thought that would be the end of Crazy Week. But something even *crazier* happened the next Monday.

We were at recess swinging on the swings when you'll never guess in a million hundred years who showed up on the playground.

No, it wasn't Mrs. Lizzy.

I *told* you that you wouldn't be able to guess. So nah-nah-nah boo-boo on you.

Just for that, I'm not gonna tell you who it was.

Okay, okay, I'll tell you.

It was Pootie the goat!

There we were, minding our own business, when out of nowhere Pootie wandered over! It was the most amazing thing in the history of the world!

"Naaaaaaayyyyy," said Pootie the goat.

"What's that goat doing here?" asked Ryan.

"She must have escaped from Rent-A-Goat," I said.

Pootie the goat was making weird noises.

"I think something's wrong with Pootie," Andrea said.

"Maybe she's sick," said Emily.

"Maybe she just needs to be milked," said Neil the nude kid.

"Well, I'm not milking her," Andrea said.

"I'm not milking her," said Ryan.

"I'm not milking her," said Michael.

Nobody wanted to milk Pootie the goat.

"I say Arlo should milk her," said Andrea.

"Why?" I asked. "I milked her last time."

"That's exactly why you should milk her *this* time, Arlo," Andrea said. "You *know* how to milk a goat. We don't know what to do."

"Milk the goat! Milk the goat!" everybody started chanting.

I was faced with the hardest decision of my life. If I milked Pootie, everybody would make fun of me for sure. And if I didn't milk Pootie, well, I was afraid that she might explode and there would be milky pieces of goat all over the place.

I didn't know what to say. I didn't know what to do. I had to think fast. I was concentrating so hard that my brain hurt.

Finally, I decided that I would rather be made fun of than be covered by milky pieces of exploded goat. So I got down on my knees and did what Mrs. Lizzy told me to do.

I thought I was gonna die. But Pootie calmed down as soon as I started milking her.

"Naaaaaaayyyyy," said Pootie.

"You're good at that, A.J.," said Neil. "When you grow up, you should milk goats for a living."

"Oooooh!" Ryan said. "A.J. is milking Pootie the goat. They must be in *love*!"

"Hey A.J., when are you and Pootie gonna get married?" asked Michael.

If those guys weren't my best friends, I would hate them.

*   *   *

Well, that's pretty much what happened during Crazy Week at Ella Mentry School. I'm gonna miss Mrs. Lizzy. She may have been crazy, but she was cool. None of our *real* teachers ever showed us how to do cool stuff like yodel or do fart noises with our armpits. And she made great balloon animals. My mom really liked her Mother's Day present.

Mrs. Lizzy was right about one thing. You never know when you might have to milk a goat.

Maybe the Board of Education will cancel the Recess Enrichment Program and just let us have fun again. Maybe we'll have another lockdown. Maybe Mrs. Lizzy will cut her hair and get earmuffs. Maybe Officer Spence will stop saying the word "duty." Maybe a zombie cannibal psycho who eats kids for breakfast will escape from the loony bin. Maybe Emily's mom will use a plate instead of eating breakfast in her pajamas. Maybe they'll let Mrs. Lizzy out of the loony bin so she can finish telling us about worm poop. Maybe Pootie will go back to Rent-A-Goat. Maybe we'll be able to talk Mr. Klutz into having another Crazy Week next year.

But it won't be easy!

Turn the page to explore the wacky, screwball world of MY WEIRD SCHOOL!

IT WAS A REAL KODAK MOMENT!

You should have been there—and now you can be. Check out these priceless moments from

MY WEIRD SCHOOL DAZE!

My Weird School Daze #1:
Mrs. Dole Is Out of Control!

Everybody was freaking out because there were sparks flying all over the place. Some of the sparks were falling on the hay at the petting zoo.

"Excuse me," I said to Emily.

"What do you want, A.J.?" Emily asked, like she was all annoyed.

"I just wanted to let you know that you're on fire," I told her.

My Weird School Daze #2:
Mr. Sunny Is Funny!

"Oh no!" yelled Mr. Sunny. "He's going to hit—"

Mr. Sunny never got the chance to finish his sentence. Because at that moment Mr. Granite landed right on top of Mr. Sunny's sand castle!

BAM! Mr. Granite crushed it! I mean, it was totally flattened! Mr. Sunny's amazing sand castle looked like a big pile of sand again . . . with a pair of feet sticking out of the top.

My Weird School Daze #3:
Mr. Granite Is from Another Planet!

"Wait a minute!" Michael said. "How do we know you're not yanking our chain? Prove you're an alien!"

"Yeah," I said. "Let's see you peel off your face."

"Well . . . okay," Mr. Granite said as he put his hand under his chin. . . .

Mr. Granite pulled at his neck, and the skin started to come loose. Then he peeled off his entire face! And you'll never believe in a million hundred years what he looked like underneath.

My Weird School Daze #4:
Coach Hyatt Is a Riot!

Coach Hyatt blew her whistle.

"Line up!"

"Are we gonna pick up your car again today?" asked Neil.

"No!" the coach barked. "Today you ragamuffins are going to learn the most important part of football—how to do an end zone dance."

"A what?" asked Ryan.

"After you score a touchdown, you have to do a dance in the end zone," Coach Hyatt said.

Then Coach Hyatt showed us her end zone dance. She shook her butt, lifted a leg over her head, hopped up and down for a while, and then put her hands in the air and waved them around like a crazy person.

Coach Hyatt is a riot!

Cheer and Sing Along
with A.J. and Pals

Graduation Song!

Sung to the tune of "Pomp and Circumstance"

I'm gra-ad-u-a-ting,

There's a square on my head.

Why is there a square on my head?

Be-cause I'm grad-u-a-ting.

Mr. Hynde's Out-of-His-Mind Rap!

Old Mr. Loring he was over the hill

So the board of education told him he would have
    to chill.

My name is Hynde, and I'm gonna blow your
    mind.

I ain't no music teacher, I'm a born music
    creature.

Cause my daddy's name was Amos, but he never
    became famous.

So he took me on his lap, and he taught me how
    to rap.

I can rhyme any line. I got juice like Dr. Seuss.

Until I hit it big, I got this teaching gig.

So sit back on your pants and dig my new break
    dance.

Root for Ella Mentry School's Pee Wee Football Team—the Moose!

That's all right! That's okay!

We're gonna win it anyway!

Go . . . Moose!

A.J.'s Guide to Yay! Vs. Boo!

Yay!

Bonbons

Summer

Recess

Calculators

Dirt bikes

Boo!

School

Crybabies

Tofu

Andrea